This

TWO HOOTS

book belongs to

....

FOR THEA
x x

First published 2020 by Two Hoots

This edition published 2021 by Two Hoots

an imprint of Pan Macmillan

The Smithson, 6 Briset Street, London EC1M 5NR

Associated companies throughout the world

www.panmacmillan.com

ISBN 978-1-5098-8985-3

Text and illustrations copyright © Morag Hood 2020

Moral rights asserted.

1 3 5 7 9 8 6 4 2

A CIP catalogue record for this book is available from the British Library.

Printed in China

The illustrations in this book were painted in gouache and then digitally coloured.

www.twohootsbooks.com

MORAG HOOD
SPAGHETTI HUNTERS

TWO HOOTS

Duck was looking for his spaghetti.

It was not going well.

"For I am the greatest spaghetti hunter there has ever been and I shall save the day."

"Spaghetti is the trickiest of all the pastas," said Tiny Horse.

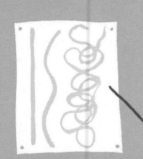

"It can be almost impossible to find."

And so the Great Spaghetti Hunt began.

It was a bit
different to how
Duck had imagined.

"I know what I'm
doing," said Tiny Horse.

"SPAGHETTI!"

Duck did not remember spaghetti
being quite so green or stringy,
and he especially did not like the
way it was hissing at him.

"NONE OF THESE
ARE SPAGHETTI!"

said Duck.

"Not even close. This one
is an **EARWIG**."

"I'm going back to my teapot."

And Duck stomped off to find a book to read.

"Books are not as good as
spaghetti," said Tiny Horse,

who had come along even though
no-one had invited her.

But this book was a bit different.

Tiny Horse was not impressed.

"This is not standard spaghetti
hunting equipment," she said.

"You can't just MAKE spaghetti."

"It does look, taste and feel a bit like spaghetti," said Tiny Horse.

"BUT NEVER FEAR!"

said Tiny Horse.

"FOR I SHALL HUNT DOWN THAT MOST FEARSOME OF BEASTS..."

"TOMATO SAUCE."

How to Make Pasta

Ingredients
300g plain flour
3 eggs

Serves four humans
(or one very hungry
duck and a tiny horse)

1. Measure the flour into a bowl.

2. Make a well in the middle of the flour and crack the eggs into it.

3. Using a fork, beat the eggs until they are smooth adding a little bit of the flour from the edge at a time. Keep going until all the egg is mixed in – you may need to use your hands to pull it all together at the end.

4. Knead the dough – pull it, bash it, stretch it and squash it! If it gets too sticky add a little flour. After 5 to 10 minutes the dough will start to feel smooth and silky.

5. Wrap your dough in cling film and pop it in the fridge to rest for thirty minutes or so.

6. Use a rolling pin to roll out the pasta. Or if you have one, use a pasta machine to get the pasta as thin as possible. Cut into any shape and leave to dry for a few minutes.

7. With the help of an adult, cook the pasta in boiling water for around 3 to 5 minutes depending on the thickness — it won't take as long as dried shop-bought pasta to cook.

Don't forget to ask an adult to help!

Add your favourite sauce and enjoy!